P9-DWI-401

Dear Parent:
Your child's love of reading starts here!

Every child learns to read in a different way and at his or her own speed. Some go back and forth between reading levels and read favorite books again and again. Others read through each level in order. You can help your young reader improve and become more confident by encouraging his or her own interests and abilities. From books your child reads with you to the first books he or she reads alone, there are I Can Read Books for every stage of reading:

SHARED READING
Basic language, word repetition, and whimsical illustrations, ideal for sharing with your emergent reader

BEGINNING READING
Short sentences, familiar words, and simple concepts for children eager to read on their own

READING WITH HELP
Engaging stories, longer sentences, and language play for developing readers

READING ALONE
Complex plots, challenging vocabulary, and high-interest topics for the independent reader

ADVANCED READING
Short paragraphs, chapters, and exciting themes for the perfect bridge to chapter books

I Can Read Books have introduced children to the joy of reading since 1957. Featuring award-winning authors and illustrators and a fabulous cast of beloved characters, I Can Read Books set the standard for beginning readers.

A lifetime of discovery begins with the magical words **"I Can Read!"**

Visit www.icanread.com for information on enriching your child's reading experience.

JUST PICK US, PLEASE!

BY MERCER MAYER

HARPER
An Imprint of HarperCollins*Publishers*

For animal shelters everywhere,
which give our furry friends new hope.

Little Critter: Just Pick Us, Please!

 For information address HarperCollins Children's Books, a division of HarperCollins Publishers, 195 Broadway, New York, NY 10007.
www.icanread.com

Library of Congress Control Number: 2017938995

ISBN 978-0-06-243143-1 (trade bdg.) — ISBN 978-0-06-243142-4 (pbk.)

17 18 19 20 21 SCP 10 9 8 7 6 5 4 3 2 1 ❖ First Edition

A Big Tuna Trading Company, LLC/J. R. Sansevere Book
www.littlecritter.com

SPECIAL
ADOPTION
PAPER
FOR....
FLORIDA
ORANGES
BIG
SPECIAL
ADOPTION
PAPER
FOR....

Gator has a new puppy.

“Where did you get it?” I ask.

“The animal shelter,” he says.

“Do they have more pets?” I ask.

“Tons and bunches,” says Gator.

That gives me an idea!

I call the critter club for a meeting.

Everyone loves my idea.

At the critter club meeting
we draw up plans and eat snacks.

Next we meet with the principal.

We ask to have a fair.
The principal likes our plan.

We show our plans to
the Critter Animal Shelter.
They love our idea.

We make flyers about
the Pet Adoption Fair.
We hang them everywhere.

We set up everything outside.
There are pens for the pets,
for dogs, cats, and more.

Everyone helps to get ready.
Mrs. Gator bakes tasty cookies.
My mom brings a big cake.

A big truck pulls up.
It is full of pets
that need homes.

The animal shelter critters
bring the pets off the truck.

We are ready.
It is time for everyone to come.
We wait and we wait.

The pets are sad.
We are sad, too.
Not many critters come.

Then all at once
everyone comes.

We are happy.
The pets are happy.

I call through a loudspeaker,
"Adopt a pet and get
special pet adoption papers."

There are big pets to adopt.
There are medium pets to adopt.
There are little pets to adopt.

There are furry pets.
There are scaly pets.
There are prickly pets.

There are pets with shells.
There are pets with horns.
There are pets with beaks.

My sister finds a cute kitten.

I find the perfect puppy.

Mom says, “No!”

"You both already have pets.
It's someone else's turn
to take one home."

A bunny and her brother are sad because we picked the pets they wanted.

We give them the kitten
and the puppy.
They are so happy.

When everyone gets picked,
we go home.
Our pets are happy to see us.

I say, "You are our pets.
We picked you already."

And they picked us, too.